NIGHT OF THE ALIENS

NIGHT OF THE ALIENS

Dayle Campbell Gaetz

Cover illustration by Lawrence B. Stilwell

To Cara

Best Wishes from

Dayle Campbell Gaetz

Roussan Publishers Inc. acknowledges with appreciation the assistance of the
Book Publishing Industry Development Program of Canadian Heritage and the
Canada Council in the production of this book.

Legal deposit 3rd quarter 1995
National Library of Canada
Quebec National Library

Canadian Cataloguing in Publication Data

**Gaetz, Dayle, 1947-
Night of the Aliens**

**(Out of this world series)
ISBN 1-896184-08-1**

**High interest-low vocabulary books. I. Title
II. Series**

**PS8563.A25317N54 1995 jC813'.54 C95-900839-X
PR9199.3.G243N54 1995**

Design by Dan Clark

Published simultaneously in Canada and the United States of America.
Printed in Canada

DEDICATION

With thanks to my son, Brian, for the inspiration.

ONE

My mother zipped up her jacket. "Now, Mark, don't do anything stupid while we're out," she warned me.

"Who, me? Come on, Mom, you know me better than that!"

She sighed and glanced at my father.

"Just don't," he said. "And don't leave a mess in the kitchen."

"Are you kidding? Have you ever known me to make a mess?"

My mother stared at me. There was a little frown between her eyebrows, as if she couldn't quite believe what she had just heard. My father folded his arms and opened his mouth to say something. I knew exactly what he would say: "Mark, you're fourteen years old. When I was your age . . ."

I had to stop him. "Don't worry about it! Just go. Have a nice dinner. When you get back, the kitchen will be spotless. Cleaner than it is now! I promise!"

At last they walked out the door. I watched the car pull out of the carport and roll down the driveway. The headlights lit up the road in front and the small redtail lights flickered through the trees. They were gone. I had the whole house to myself. Great! All I wanted to do was relax and watch the hockey game. I was very tired from playing in a volleyball tournament all week.

After mixing up some chocolate milk I made a nutritious

supper—two peanut butter and tomato sandwiches with a slice of cheese and a little lettuce for flavour. To go with them I opened a tin of smoked oysters. My dog followed me into the living room with his nose twitching in the air. He's crazy about oysters.

"Ahh," I said, settling back in my dad's recliner. "Now we can relax, eh, Wimp?"

The game was about to start, I flicked on the TV. Wimp settled beside the chair, grinning up at me and drooling. I popped an oyster into my mouth and was choosing one for Wimp when a brilliant white light burst into the room. I gulped and the oyster caught in my throat. I started coughing. I couldn't stop. I coughed so hard I thought my eyes would pop right out of my head. Finally the oyster shot back into my mouth and I spit it out. I didn't feel like oysters any more.

I reached for my chocolate milk. Glancing down, I saw that Wimp had stuck his nose under the chair, like he always does when he's scared. But the bright light was long gone by then.

I drank some chocolate milk and glanced nervously toward the windows. They take up one whole wall of our living room and below them our front yard slopes down to a dirt road. On the other side of the road is a wide open field and a swamp. There aren't any other houses in sight—no lights, nothing. So where had the white light come from?

I wanted to get up and take a closer look but I couldn't get out of the chair without breaking Wimp's nose. So I leaned over with the oyster tin in my hand, trying to lure him out. Wimp just whimpered and tried to get farther under the chair. Then the Canucks scored and I forgot all about the flash of light.

I had one bite of sandwich left and a Mighty Duck was on a breakaway when the TV went fuzzy. A huge ball of fire shot past the windows, hurling brilliant white light into the room. A high-pitched, whining sound went with it.

"Okay Wimp," I said after it had gone, "let's show a little courage here. Let's go and check it out. It's probably just a truck with a searchlight on it."

Wimp crawled into the corner behind the recliner and looked up at me as if he didn't understand English.

I got out of the chair. "Come on, Wimp. You're supposed to be the watchdog around here."

He closed his eyes. You might be thinking Wimp is a toy poodle or a little spaniel. Wrong! He's a big German shepherd. He looks like he could tear you to pieces. But I've seen rabbits that are braver than him.

So, I was on my own. Turning the TV sound off, I walked out the door onto the front porch.

The silence was eerie. There were no cars or trucks on the road and no planes in the sky. Black outlines of the tall pines in our front yard stood hushed against the moonlit sky.

As I watched, the branches began to move, slowly at first and then faster, swishing against each other. A cold wind brushed across my face. My hair stood on end. Then I heard it–a high pitched whine somewhere in the distance. It was getting louder by the second. I ran inside, slammed the door, and leaned against it. The living room windows lit up with a light so bright I had to close my eyes. A whine, like a giant mosquito, filled my ears.

The whining stopped, the microwave beeped five times and

the sound came back on the TV. Reaching behind my back, I locked the door. Then, hunched forward at the waist, I hurried into the living room to turn off the TV. "Let's go!" I whispered.

Wimp didn't move until I reached the kitchen and opened the door to the basement. Then he raced toward me with his ears back, as if a ghost were on his tail. I stepped out of the way as he charged down the stairs.

At one end of the basement is a half-finished room. It isn't fancy but it's mine. My weight set is in there and some old furniture and a TV.

By the time I got to the room Wimp had squeezed himself between a chair and the couch. He put his paws over his eyes. Picking up my baseball bat, I checked that the door to the carport was locked. Then I switched on the TV with the volume down low so I would be able to hear if anything happened. Clutching the bat, I settled down to watch the game.

By the end of the first period nothing weird had happened. Even Wimp relaxed. He moved into the middle of the room and flopped on his side like there was nothing to worry about.

I was starting to get hungry. I couldn't stop thinking about fresh, hot popcorn with butter melting into it. I licked my lips. "Come on Wimp," I said. "Whatever was out there must be gone by now."

Wimp stood up, stretched, and followed me up the stairs. Maybe, I told myself, I had been imagining things. I had probably been watching too much TV, like my mother always says. Or maybe I had fallen asleep and dreamed the whole thing. Anyway, I carried my baseball bat with me. Not that I was scared or anything, it's just that I like to be prepared.

The kitchen windows face the road, the same as the living room. But they have thick curtains and I closed them before switching on the light. I poured popcorn into the popper and plugged it in. It makes a loud, whirring noise, so, as soon as it started up, Wimp ran out of the kitchen. I put butter into a bowl and was carrying it toward the microwave when, for no reason, the microwave beeped, five times. I froze.

The windows, right through the curtains, were ablaze with light. My stomach flipped over. I turned around just as the top burst off the popcorn popper. It landed right in my arms. I almost dropped the bowl of melted butter. Melted butter!

I hadn't put it into the microwave yet, but it was melted. I stuck my finger into the yellow liquid and jerked it out again. Hot!

By that time popcorn was shooting out of the machine and flying all over the kitchen. It was like a hailstorm in there. I ran over and tried to catch some of the popcorn but most of it shot up into the air and came down on the counter, the floor, and the table. In the living room Wimp started barking.

"It's okay Wimp," I called. "It's just popcorn. It won't hurt you."

But he wouldn't stop. When the last piece of popcorn shot out and landed on the floor, the machine shut itself off. That's when I noticed another noise over Wimp's barking. It sounded like a hockey game in our living room.

I started running but my feet shot out from under me. I landed face down in the popcorn and my head bumped against the floor.

I sat up, rubbing my forehead. My head hurt as I got up. I shuffled out of the kitchen, shoveling a path through the popcorn with my feet. In the living room, Wimp was still barking and I realized the TV had somehow turned itself back on. I walked into the room and stopped. My heart thudded against my ribs and my mouth went dry.

Someone was sitting in my father's chair!

TWO

My chin fell just about to my knees. I opened my mouth to yell, "What are you doing in my house?" but only a weird croak came out, as if someone had their hands around my throat.

The person in the chair looked up. She had silver hair and eyes as green as the sea. She was wearing a silver jump suit with high shoulder pads and a wide shiny belt. The whole suit seemed to glow with its own light. On the carpet beside the chair was a silver helmet, the same shape as my trail bike helmet, with a clear faceplate.

"Hello," the woman said. Most people smile when they say hello. This woman didn't smile, but she didn't exactly look angry either. She looked--worried. She stood up and took a step toward me. I jumped back.

What the heck was she doing here? Maybe she got lost on her way to a Halloween party. But this was the middle of November.

Okay, I had it. She was not only lost but two weeks late as well. "I think you have the wrong house," my voice squeaked.

"I do not think so." She took my hand and shook it. Her grip was so strong my bones rubbed together. "I am Madra," she said. "We have come for you."

"We?" I rolled my eyes sideways to look for more of them.

"Yes," she said. "We need you to help save the people of our planet."

Oh my God! I thought. There's a crazy lady loose in my house. What am I going to do with her?

"Of course," I said gently. "I'll be glad to help. I just need to make a little phone call first."

I turned and bolted for the kitchen. Wimp was right in front of me, his tail between his legs. We hit the kitchen at a run. Should I ask for the police or an ambulance. If only I had remembered the popcorn!

I was reaching for the phone when I lost my footing. I'm still not quite sure whether it was Wimp or the popcorn that tripped me. Maybe it was Wimp sliding on the popcorn. Whatever happened, the next thing I knew I was sprawled on the floor with the dog underneath me. He narrowed his eyes at me as if I had purposely tripped him.

When I looked up, the silver-haired woman was standing beside the phone. She crossed her arms and studied my face.

"Believe it or not," she said. "I am not crazy."

"Of course not," I grinned, getting to my feet and brushing pieces of popcorn off my jeans. "Why would anyone think that?"

"We have been watching you, Mark."

I gulped. She knew my name! But then I remembered my name was on the mug I used for my chocolate milk. It was still sitting on the end table beside my father's chair. The problem now was to distract her so I could get to the phone. "Did you have anything to do with that ball of light?" I asked gently.

She stared at me, her green eyes seemed to bore right into my brain. "Oh, you mean the explorer. That was the kids. They wanted to have a look at you before we picked you up. So they

14

took turns driving past."

"Kids?"

She nodded. "Young people really, about your age. They are very curious. I hope you were not too frightened?"

"Who, me?" I shook my head and laughed. "Not at all!"

"I thought maybe you were when you moved downstairs." I gulped. How did she know about that? "No. I just moved because this TV wasn't working right."

"Oh, yes. I am sorry. I warned them to be careful. Sometimes we cause a power surge if we come too close. It can make your electricity do strange things."

She had not moved away from the phone. I glanced at the baseball bat, lying on the counter beside it. "Well," I said, taking a step closer, "how do you like Earth so far?"

"Earth?" she looked confused. "Oh, you mean your planet, Neerg."

"Sure, I guess so."

"I have visited here many times," she said. "You must understand, there are not many of us left up on Detsaw. We are searching the universe for new homes."

"I see," I answered thoughtfully. Obviously she had escaped from the nearest psych ward. There must be people out looking for her. Probably the lights I had seen were searchlights. But where could the lights have come from?

Why hadn't I heard a helicopter or a van? If I could just get her to sit down at the table, maybe I would be able to reach the phone. "Would you like some popcorn?"

She looked down at the floor. Wimp was stretched out on

the popcorn, his face between his paws, looking up at her with sad eyes.

"No, thank you," she said. "I am not really hungry."

"Chocolate milk?"

She shook her head. "I want you to come with me. My friends would like to meet you."

"Really?" I squeaked. I cleared my throat and then my voice came out really deep. "Why me?"

"We have been watching you. We need someone just like you."

The phone rang. I almost jumped out of my shoes. She picked it up and handed it to me.

"Hello?"

"Hi Mark, you watching the game?"

"Richard! Am I glad... not right now... there's a...." The woman put her hand on my shoulder. Some sort of power, like an electrical shock leaped out of it and shot straight to my brain. I forgot what I was going to say.

"Want some help with your trail bike tomorrow?"

Richard's voice seemed far away.

"Sure Richard," I said. "I gotta go now." I hung up.

"Ready for transport," said the woman.

My body went weird, as if there were needles sticking into every muscle. Then my arms and legs started jerking around, out of control.

When I looked down my feet had disappeared. Then my legs went. My hands vanished in front of my eyes. I screamed and even my scream disappeared. For a flash in time there was no me. And then I heard my scream coming back at me through space. It filled the air and echoed all around me.

My hands came back. I looked down. I still had no feet.

People were in the room, watching quietly as I screamed and jerked around like a total idiot. The woman, Madra, stood beside me with her hand still resting on my shoulder. It felt very warm.

"Do not worry," she said when I finally managed to stop screaming and jerking. Her voice was very smooth, very easy to listen to. "You will get used to transport."

"I don't want to get used to it," I shouted. "I want my feet back!"

She glanced at the floor and back up at my face. I looked down. My feet were there, same as always, in my old, ripped running shoes.

"What are you doing to me?"

"I told you," she spoke calmly, "I want you to meet my friends."

The other people in the room were whispering to each other. I couldn't see them very well because they were in the dark and I was standing in bright lights.

The room was too hot. So hot I could hardly breathe. "Are you all right?" asked Madra.

"Who, me? Of course. Why wouldn't I be? I do stuff like this all the time."

"You look a little pale. I do not want to let go of your shoulder unless I am sure you will not fall."

"Don't worry," I told her, "I'm tough." I shrugged my shoulder to get rid of her hand. She let go. I collapsed.

THREE

When I opened my eyes I was looking up at a rounded ceiling. I turned my head and saw that I was lying on a narrow bed in a small, white room. Above my head the walls curved inward to form a dome, like an igloo. I tried to sit up.

"Oh, you are awake!" said a girl with a round, serious face and short brown hair. She was slim but strong looking, and wore a pure white jumpsuit.

"Where am I?"

"In Recovery One," she said.

With my hands I felt the thick strap across my chest. I tried to move my legs but they were strapped down too.

"Am I a prisoner?" I asked her.

She frowned. "We do not take prisoners."

"Then why the heck am I tied down?"

"So that you will not hurt yourself. It is a shock to the system the first time one is transported."

Transported. She had me there, I definitely was not in my kitchen any more. "So, how do you do that anyway?"

She shrugged. "I am not a scientist. Do you know how your fax machines work?"

"FAX!" I struggled to break loose. "You mean I'm not really me? I'm just a copy? Are there two of me now? Which one is real?"

Her eyes opened wide and she stared at me. I noticed how

green her eyes were. As green as the sea, just like Madra's. Then she threw back her head and laughed. She laughed so hard I thought she would fall over. "I am sorry," she said, trying to stop.

"What's so funny?" I asked crossly.

She stopped laughing and put her hands against her cheeks. A look of surprise came over her face. "I do not know," she said. "I have never done that before. It feels very strange--but quite pleasant."

I turned my face away but studied her out of the corner of my eye.

She took a step closer, biting her lip. "Do not worry, you are not a copy. I did not explain very well. What I meant was that you probably cannot tell me how a fax machine works. Or how a telephone works. In the same way I cannot tell you how a transporter works. It just does."

I liked the way she talked. She sounded like someone who had just learned to speak English. Also, she looked kind of pretty now that her face was flushed pink from laughing.

"Are you going to undo these stupid straps?" I asked her.

"Soon," she said. "I must get the doctor first." She walked away.

"Wait! You didn't tell me your name."

She stopped. "I am Kaylin," she said, "I will see you later." The double doors slid open and she was gone.

***

Soon after Kaylin left, the doors slid open again. A tall, thin man in a white coat and white pants walked in.

"Hello," he said. "I am Dr. Senob. Are you feeling better?"

"I'll be just great as soon as you untie me."

"Certainly." He undid the chest strap and I sat up. He checked my heartbeat and breathing. His hands were warm, which was strange, I thought all doctors had cold hands. I started undoing the leg strap. "Look," I said, "I don't know who you people are or what you did to me. I'm not sure how you got me here--I don't even know where I am! But you can't keep me prisoner. I want to go home."

"Prisoner?" he said, "we do not take prisoners." He frowned, just the way Kaylin had done.

That's when I noticed his eyes. They were as green as Kaylin's and Madra's. There was something very weird about these people.

"So I can go home now?" I slid off the stretcher and stood facing him.

He shook his head. "Not yet. You are a guest. There is much to do." He swung around and walked toward the doors. They slid open.

"But I don't want to be a guest!" I ran after him. The doors slid shut in front of my nose. I put both hands flat on one of the doors, trying to slide it open. They were like elevator doors but made of a shiny, silver metal. I tried to get my fingers between them and pry them open. They wouldn't budge. I checked out the walls beside the doors but there were no buttons to push. Finally I just stood still, thinking things through. Dr. Senob had not touched anything. He had walked across the floor and the doors had opened for him. The same with Kaylin. I tried stepping exactly where they had stepped.

Nothing happened.

"Prisoner?" I said, frowning like Kaylin and Dr. Senob. "We do not take prisoners." Their faces looked so innocent with those wide green eyes. Madra too. I wondered what they wanted from me.

Maybe they were some kind of mad scientists who had kidnapped me to use in experiments. For some reason they wanted me to think they were from another planet. And they were doing a good job of it--I remembered how my body had disappeared. Madra must have hypnotized me. Okay, that made sense. I put my hand to my forehead and my fingers touched something-- a bandage! It ran from one side of my head to the other.

"Ahhh!" I screamed and ran to the doors, pounding on them with both fists. I pulled my leg back, determined to kick the doors down. My foot swung forward; the doors slid open. Kaylin was standing there holding a tray of food. Her green eyes widened as my foot whipped up and caught the bottom of the tray. It flew out of her hands and clattered to the ground followed by the sound of breaking glass.

Kaylin just stood there with a puzzled look on her face. "Why did you do that?" she finally asked.

"I know what you're up to. And I'm getting out of here!"

She was a little shorter than me. Her big, green eyes stared up into mine. I couldn't move. "What are we up to?" she asked.

"Experiments." I touched the bandage. "You did something to my head."

"Poor Mark." She put her hand on my shoulder. It felt warm and totally relaxing.

"You fell and bumped your head," she told me. "Dr. Senob bandaged it."

"He didn't take anything out?"

"Out? Like what?"

"Like... part of my brain."

She let go of my shoulder and rubbed her hand across her forehead. "I am sure he did not," she said. But she squinted up at me as if she thought part of my brain really had gone missing.

"Are you going to let me out of here, or do I have to fight my way out?" I raised my fists.

She frowned. "If you want, I will show you the rest of the ship."

"Ship? We're on a ship? Where are you taking me? Iraq? Ireland? I knew it all along! You're terrorists, aren't you?"

She bit her lip. "No. We are making a special visit to Detsaw. We want you to see our planet."

"Oh sure. Back to the home planet. Just for me. How kind of you!"

Kaylin crouched down and started picking little bits of glass out of a brown puddle.

"That looks like chocolate milk," I said.

"It is."

I picked up one of the sandwiches. Peanut butter, cheese, lettuce and tomato. I looked around. Sure enough there was a small, flat tin lying upside down in a pool of oil. Greenish brown lumps

22

were scattered all around it: smoked oysters.

"We wanted you to feel at home," Kaylin explained.

***

"OK," I said when everything had been cleaned up, "let's go on this tour."

We walked down a narrow hallway made all of metal. It had a curved ceiling that wasn't far above my head. There were doors off both sides of it. Kaylin turned toward a door and it slid open. I couldn't figure out how she did it.

The room we stepped into had shelves of books. Small tables were scattered about, like in a school library. Three teenagers were sitting at a table, talking quietly. They all wore pure white jumpsuits like Kaylin's. Except for their clothes they looked like an ordinary group of kids that you would see at any high school. One of them was a small girl who looked Asian and had long, jet black hair. The other two were boys; one was very black with short, curly hair and the other had pale white skin, freckles and bright red hair. When the door slid closed behind us they looked up. I stopped and stared. All three of them had brilliant green eyes.

FOUR

"Everybody, this is Mark. I am taking him on a tour of the ship." They all gathered around me.

"Mark, this is Lotus, Orlando and Red." Each of them shook my hand, very formally.

"Red?"

The boy with red hair shrugged. He was about my height but very thin. "That is my nickname," he said. "My real name is Ruadhagen."

"Oh," I said. "Red's good."

All three of them started firing questions at me. "Did we scare you when we drove past your house?"

"How do you like our ship?"

"We did not mean to scare you."

"Do you like living on Neerg?"

"You are so lucky!"

"Can you teach us to play games and to laugh?"

I looked back and forth from one to the other. There was no way I could answer them when they all talked at once.

"I wasn't scared," I said when they stopped talking.

"You must teach us how to speak correctly," said Kaylin. "We must learn to fit in on your planet."

"Oh, right," I said. "I keep forgetting that you're from another planet."

"He does not believe us," Kaylin explained to her friends. "He thinks we are terrorists."

"Terrorists?" said Red, frowning.

"You know," said Lotus, "from history? Terrorists tried to get what they wanted by killing innocent people."

Orlando looked down at me; he was very tall, with broad shoulders. "We do not have time for killing on our planet."

"Very impressive," I said, folding my arms and shaking my head at the four of them. "You're all terrific actors. But I'm not buying. Now, just show me the door so I can go home."

"Come over here," said Kaylin. As she walked toward the wall, a huge panel slid open, uncovering an amazing display. A window, the size of the wall, looked out on space. Nothing but space. I ran over. Little tiny lights, like stars, floated above my head and below my feet. We were shooting through the lights so fast they spun around us like snowflakes in the headlights of a car. Stay cool, I told myself, think this through.

Then it hit me and I laughed aloud. "You'll have to do better than that!" I looked at Kaylin. Her eyes rolled toward the others. "I know a big computer screen when I see one. Do you think I'm stupid?"

Kaylin didn't answer.

"Let us take him to the exit port," suggested Red.

"Now you're getting the idea," I told him.

"Do you think he should go outside?" asked Lotus in a worried voice.

Kaylin nodded. "Yes. It would be good for him."

They led me along another hallway and we took an elevator down. We stopped in front of a door with a sign that said, *EXIT PORT CHANGE ROOM*.

"Do you really think we should do this?" asked Orlando.

"Remember, he is tough," said Red. "He can handle it."

"He did not handle transport very well," Lotus reminded him. "This is different."

The doors slid open to a long, narrow room. A row of shiny metal suits hung on pegs along each wall. On a shelf above each suit was a helmet with a face plate. And below each one was a pair of high silver boots.

"This one should fit," said Kaylin.

"Are you kidding? Do you think I'd walk down the street in that outfit? Halloween is over, remember?"

"Do not worry, no one will see you," she said.

"The doors will not open unless you are wearing a proper suit," Orlando explained.

So I pulled it on over my jeans and T-shirt. I threw off my running shoes and slipped my feet into the boots. But when Kaylin tried to put a helmet over my head I pushed it away.

"The suit is useless without the helmet," she told me. "Besides, no one will know who you are if you are wearing it."

That made sense. I didn't know where I was but I figured a building this size had to be somewhere in Kelowna, the closest city to my house. Imagine what my friends would say if they saw me in this get up. But with the helmet on, they would never recognize me, I would be just another weirdo walking the streets.

After I put on the helmet I noticed Orlando had disappeared. The other three strapped a tank on my back and Kaylin tried to close the faceplate. "Leave it open," I said. "Are you trying to gas me?"

They shook their heads like adults do when a little kid says something silly.

"These Neerg people have a lot to learn," said Lotus.

"When you are ready to come in just wave your arms like this," said Red, waving his arms in front of his face.

"You don't get it, do you? I'm not coming back," I told them. "I'm going home to get the popcorn off the floor before my parents come home." If they got there before I did I was in big trouble.

Kaylin led me to another door. The sign on it said, *EXIT PORT 2, KEEP CLOSED AT ALL TIMES*.

"When the door opens you must step inside," Kaylin explained. "I cannot go with you. You will be in a very small room. Soon you will begin to feel unusually light. Then the other door will open and you will float outside."

"Right," I chuckled. "I'll just go floating out the door like a big old blimp."

Kaylin's brow wrinkled. "You are not a blimp," she said. "Do you not know about walking in space? I understand people of Neerg have done this."

Before I could answer, the door slid open and somehow I stepped--or was pushed--through it. The room was small all right. Just big enough for one person to stand up. There was a door in front of me with a big sign that said: *EXIT PORT--FINAL*. I tried to figure out how to open it. Like all the other doors in this place it had no handles to pull or buttons to push.

I started to feel funny. My arms wouldn't stay at my sides. They floated away from me until they bumped against the sides of the little room. My stomach felt weird too; I thought I was going to be sick. But I forgot about that when my whole body lifted gently off the ground. My faceplate snapped shut just as the door opened. My head and shoulders floated out the hole. I looked down. There was nothing underneath me. I mean nothing! I tried to grab at the walls of the room but they were too smooth. I floated out the door and it closed behind me.

"Ahhh!" I screamed and kicked my legs, trying to get back to the door. But it had floated away. My heart pounded against my ribs. This was the end! I was going to die! I would be just one more piece of space junk floating around forever. No one on Earth would ever know what had happened to me.

Something tapped on my helmet. Someone was floating beside me. I squinted through his faceplate and saw that it was Orlando. This couldn't be happening. Me, floating around in space like an astronaut? It just was not possible. I had to be dreaming. Orlando touched my arm and pointed toward the ship. It was round like a huge ball and it shone bright silver. There were two long lines coming out from it. One was attached to Orlando, the other to me. Orlando spread his arms and ducked his head. He dove down and then lifted his head and started back up again. By moving his arms and legs he could swing from one side to the other. I tried it.

It was great! I went up and down and made big loops forward and backward in space. What a feeling! I could have stayed out there forever. If this were a dream I didn't want to wake up. Not yet.

I was floating upside down when Orlando came over, grabbed my arm and pointed toward the ship. He waved his arms in front of his face, like Red had shown me. Then he held onto his life line. He pointed at mine. I shook my head. He pointed at my air tank and then again at my life line. He grabbed his throat and rolled his eyes upward as if he were suffocating. I understood. If I'm not dreaming, I thought as the line started pulling me toward the ship, then... Richard will never believe this!

But, if I wasn't dreaming, would I ever get a chance to tell him?

FIVE

"Now do you believe that we are on a space ship?" asked Red.

"I guess so." My knees were shaking as I took off the silver suit. "Either that or I'm dreaming."

"Do not worry. You are not dreaming. We need your help on Detsaw."

"How could I possibly help you?"

"We will explain," said Orlando. "But first let us go and get something to eat."

That was the best idea I had heard for hours.

The five of us went back up in the elevator together. Stepping out, I walked beside Kaylin along short hallways, turning left and right and left again. All the doors slid open as we got to them.

"How do you do that?" I asked Kaylin.

"Do what?"

"Open the doors."

She shrugged. "They are heat sensitive."

"Heat sensitive?"

She nodded. "They open automatically."

"Then why won't they open for me?"

She put her hand on my arm. "Have you not noticed?" she asked. "You are cold." I felt the heat from her hand on my arm and remembered how warm Madra's hand had been on my shoulder. The doctor's hands were warm too. I swung

29

around. Lotus was behind me. I put my hand on her cheek. She was very warm, like someone with a high fever. I tried Orlando–hot! And then Red– oh man! Panic Time! I put my hands to my own face. It was cold, like a dead fish. Then I saw myself floating out the door marked, *EXIT PORT – FINAL.*

"Oh my God!" I gasped. "I'm not dreaming! It all makes sense now. I'm dead. That's it! I must be dead!" The four of them stood still, staring at me, their eyes wide.

"What happened?" I shouted, throwing my hands in the air. Suddenly I felt so bad I wished I was dead. No I didn't. I wished I was alive! "My poor parents!" I moaned, beating my fists against the wall. "I'm their only son! What will they do? I don't want to die!"

I went up to Kaylin and put my hands on her shoulders. "You've got to tell me, what did I die of? Oh, my God! I slapped my hand against my bandaged forehead. "I must have choked on a smoked oyster. What a way to go!" None of them moved while I was jumping around and yelling. Finally I stopped and looked at them standing there with their cool green eyes and pure white suits. The truth hit me. "So," I said quietly, "are you angels?"

They looked at each other. Orlando started laughing first. Then the others joined in. My jaw dropped open as I watched them. What was so blasted funny?

"Mad. . .," Lotus said, gasping for air. "Mad. . .," she tried again but doubled over. At last she blurted out, "Madra made a good choice!"

The others nodded, laughing until tears streamed from their eyes.

I could have died. That is, if I wasn't already. One thing I really hate is being laughed at. I should be used to it though. My father keeps telling me, "Think before you act." But I always get it backward. I always act before I think. Well, no more, from now on I would be very careful. I would never speak without thinking first. Maybe I would never speak at all.

***

When they could walk without breaking up, they took me into the kitchen. It was all silver and white, but no bigger than our kitchen at home. The four of them set to work grating cheese, chopping vegetables, and stirring something in the microwave. Pretty soon there was a big platter of food on the table, full of cheese and noodles. It smelled great.

We all filled our plates. I had eaten almost half of mine when Red said, "Are dead people supposed to eat?"

"I do not think so," said Kaylin and she pulled my plate away.

"You are right," said Lotus. "We should not waste our good food on a dead person."

"But I'm hungry!" I pulled back my plate. "I can't be dead if I'm hungry." So much for never speaking again.

"Too bad," said Orlando. "I was going to finish yours for you."

"Thanks a lot," I said.

When I had eaten it all I leaned back in my chair. "So, if I'm not dead and I'm not dreaming and you guys are for real, why am I here?"

"We told you, we need your help."

"Why me?"

"Madra says we are much too serious," said Kaylin. "She says we need to learn how to laugh."

"And you are funny," said Red. "We have already learned that lesson."

I glared at him.

"We need to learn how to act like the young people on Neerg," Lotus told me. "We need to fit in."

"Why?"

"Our planet is too warm now. Once it was like your planet, but Detsaw got too crowded, we cut down too many trees. Now the land is wasted and we cannot live there for much longer."

"We are moving as many people as we can," Orlando explained. "They are being taken to every planet that has people living on it. We were sent to Neerg to find someone who could teach our people how to fit in on your planet."

"We have observed that people on your planet are very cruel to those who are different," added Lotus. "So we must learn to be like you."

I shook my head sadly. "Boy did you get the wrong guy! Everyone laughs at me because I can never do anything right! Even you laugh at me! What you need is someone really cool."

Kaylin touched my hand with her warm fingers. "You are very cool," she said.

I sighed. These people had a lot to learn.

***

After eating we went back to the library and sat at a round table. "How did you learn to speak English?" I asked.

"The computer taught us."

"Oh, that explains it."

"Explains what?" asked Red.

"It explains the way you talk. See, we always say 'don't' instead of 'do not'. And 'won't' instead of 'will not'. We have lots of words like that."

"I have noticed that you speak differently," said Kaylin. "Please teach us."

We sat around talking for hours. I told them what it was like to live on Earth and they told me how sad they were to leave their home. While we talked, they practiced speaking the way most kids back home would speak. They learned quickly.

Something was still bothering me. "Won't it take years to get to your planet?" I asked them.

"It would if we took the long way," said Lotus. "We would all be old before we got home. But we have found a way to take short cuts through space."

"It is–it's—hard to explain," said Orlando. "Only the scientists really understand. But it's like building a bridge across a river so you do n... don't have to go all the way around. Only it's a bridge through space."

"We'll be there tomorrow," said Kaylin. "You must teach the people everything you know before they leave for Neerg."

33

"How many are going?"

"Hundreds will be moving to your country. We have noticed that your country is less crowded than the rest of your planet. Also, there are many different races of people living there, so we should fit it more easily."

Imagine me, teaching hundreds of people everything I know. I tried to think of something I could teach them. I tried to think of something I knew. I wanted to tell them more about Earth but I hadn't seen very much of it. I couldn't tell them about history because I had never paid much attention in school. I shook my head. This wasn't going to work.

"I still say you picked the wrong guy. See? I don't know anything."

"That's okay," Kaylin patted my hand. "We didn't choose you because you are smart."

"Thanks, that makes me feel a lot better."

She laughed.

***

That night I settled on a bunk in a small room that I shared with Red and Orlando.

"How come we haven't seen any other people on the ship?" I asked.

"There aren't very many," Red told me. "This is a shuttle – it's small and fast. It doesn't need a big crew to run it."

"We are most of the crew," Orlando added. "Most days we have to work. But Madra gave us today off so we could get to know you."

34

"Where is Madra?"

"She spends most of her time on the flight deck. She's the captain, you know."

"Oh," I said, "she didn't tell me."

I lay on my bunk with my hands behind my head, staring into the darkness and listening to the quiet hum of the ship. I wondered what my parents were doing, they must have come home by now and found the popcorn all over the floor. At first they would be mad, then they would probably notice I wasn't there. They would start to worry. I still couldn't believe this was happening. I kept expecting to wake up suddenly and discover I had been dreaming. But I knew now, if I did wake up, I would be disappointed. I closed my eyes. Someone was snoring. The next thing I heard was a loud, screaming siren. I shook myself awake. The smoke alarm, I thought, it's the smoke alarm outside my room. So, I was home, in my own bed, the dream was over. I sat up.

"Ouch!" I bumped my head on the bunk above me. The light came on. Red and Orlando were zipping up their jumpsuits. The siren faded away.

"Put this on," said Red, throwing a white suit at me.

I did as I was told. "What's going on?" I asked them.

"It's an emergency. We don't know what yet. We've got to go to the flight deck."

"Follow us!" said Red as they ran out the door.

35

SIX

As we ran down the hallways every door slid open so fast we didn't even need to slow down. Kaylin and Lotus ran into the elevator behind us.

"Do you know what happened?" asked Red.

"No," said Lotus. "But it must be pretty bad. Madra has never used the emergency alert before. Not even when we almost hit that meteor on the way to Neerg."

A chill shot down my spine. I opened my mouth to shout, "We're all going to die!" But I snapped it shut in time. They had enough to worry about without me making it worse. The elevator doors opened and we stepped into a room filled with instrument panels and computer screens. The room was shaped like an upside down bowl, and it was nearly all made of glass. I stopped, amazed.

From waist height up to the top of the dome, there was wide open space. The light of stars was so far away we seemed to be just floating there, not moving at all. The others had rushed over to the computer monitor by Madra where they were talking quietly together. I hurried over to join my new friends. As I got there they all turned around and looked out through the glass dome behind Madra.

"I think I see it!" said Orlando. "Look," he pointed, "right there!"

"I think it's your imagination," Red told him.

"No, wait, I see something too," said Kaylin. "It's getting brighter!"

I looked in the same direction, even though I didn't know what I was looking for.

"There it is!" said Lotus. "It looks like a bright star."

I searched back and forth through space. After a few minutes I noticed that one star did seem a little brighter than the others. I kept my eyes on it. "What is it?" I asked.

"An attack ship," said Lotus. "From the planet Sloof."

"Sloof?" I chuckled. "Are you kidding? That sounds like a cartoon."

"Cartoon?" Lotus looked up at me, her forehead wrinkled.

The others all stared at me as if I had said something stupid.

"Cartoon," I repeated. "Funny drawings and words that make you laugh. On TV the drawings move around and talk, just like real people."

They looked at each other. Kaylin shrugged. "There's nothing funny about the Sloof," she said. "And right now, we've got to get busy or they'll kill us all."

"They are closing in," said Madra. "We have reached top speed but they are still gaining. Zared is trying to contact them but they refuse to answer. We must assume that they are planning to attack without warning."

On the far side of the room, a man was working at a computer keyboard. He was dark, but not as dark as Orlando. He was wearing earphones, his head was bent and he didn't take notice of any of us.

Madra turned away from her computer screen. "Lotus and Red, close the shields over the dome and check that all windows in the ship are shielded. Orlando, activate our defense system. Kaylin, I want you to monitor the Sloof ship's progress. Figure out exactly how long we have before the attack."

Everyone ran to do their jobs and I stood there feeling like a fool. I watched as panel after panel slid up to cover the dome. Kaylin was working away at a computer so I walked over and stood behind her. On the screen were a whole bunch of numbers.

'What are you doing?" I asked her.

"I'm figuring out our speed and the Sloof ship's speed. Then I'm calculating the distance between us. In a few minutes I'll know how long we have."

I gulped. "To live?"

She glanced up at me. "Until the attack."

Not far from her, Orlando was working at another computer.

"So," I said. "I guess you're going to blow these guys out of space."

"No," said Orlando. "That's the first lesson we learned when we found out our planet was in danger. We no longer fight or kill."

"But–what about your defense system? Don't you have any weapons?"

"No. We have ways of avoiding their weapons and we have protective shields. Our defense should work against most attacks."

"Should? Most? You mean they sometimes don't work?"

"We don't know yet," said Orlando. "We've never had to use them before."

"Well," I said. "That's cool. You finally have a chance to test them."

"Ten minutes until attack," said Kaylin.

"All the window shields are locked in place," Lotus reported.

"Good," said Madra. "Now, make a visual check of the ship. Every room, starting with the kitchen. Be sure there is nothing loose that can cause damage."

Lotus and Red ran out the door.

"Zared, have you made contact with Detsaw?"

"Yes. They confirm the Sloof ship plans to attack. The Sloof want to destroy our last shuttle because they want Neerg for themselves."

"Advise space traffic control we may need assistance after re-entry."

I walked over to Madra. "Why do they want to stop you?" I asked her. "Isn't there enough room for both of your people on my planet?"

"You do not understand," she said. "These people have already blown up their own planet with their foolish weapons. Only a few hundred Sloof have survived and they are living on a space platform until they find a new home. They are cruel, greedy people who would take over your world and make slaves of your people. We are the only ones who can teach your people how to defend themselves from the Sloof weapons."

"But we have weapons too."

"Yes, you do. But if you use them you will destroy your own world."

"Five minutes until attack!" said Kaylin.

My stomach turned upside down.

"Mark," said Madra. "I want you to sit in the chair next to Kaylin. She will show you how to strap yourself in before the attack."

Kaylin had already strapped herself in when I got there. I sat down and she showed me how the seatbelts fit across my shoulders and legs.

"'Four minutes until attack!" she called. Then, to me she said, "Reach under the seat and find your helmet."

I lifted up a helmet that looked a lot like the ones in the exit port change room. A hose ran out of it and was attached to something under the seat.

"Practice putting it on," she said. "It fits tightly to your suit and it will give you oxygen if you need it." While I was putting it on she called out, "Three minutes until attack."

The helmet sucked itself down tight over the neck of my suit. I wondered how you turned on the oxygen. I looked around for a switch but I couldn't see one anywhere. There wasn't much air in the helmet. I was already having trouble breathing so I decided to take it off. I reached up and pulled. It didn't move. I tried twisting it to one side. It wouldn't budge. Kaylin was busy checking the numbers on her screen.

"Kaylin," I said. She didn't hear me.

"Kaylin!" I yelled. Still she didn't hear me.

By then I was gasping for air and my heart was pounding inside my chest. I tapped Kaylin on the shoulder. When she turned I made a face at her, holding my hands at my throat. She took both of my hands and placed them on the sides of the helmet where there were two switches. I flipped them up and the helmet came loose.

40

"Sorry," she said. "I forgot about you."

"I could have died!"

She shook her head. "The oxygen comes on automatically. The only time you might be in trouble is if you panicked."

"Who, me? Panic? Maybe this helmet isn't working."

"Orlando checked all of them while you were talking to Madra."

"Oh."

"One minute until attack!"

"What happened to two?"

"You were in the helmet. By the way, there's a switch under your chin that lets you talk and hear."

I saw that Orlando, Zared and Madra had strapped themselves to their chairs. The elevator doors opened. Lotus and Red hurried in. Right behind them was Dr. Senob carrying his bag. All three of them sat down and strapped themselves in.

"Are you sure they'll just attack without warning?" asked Kaylin.

"Yes," said Zared. "They have already warned space traffic control on Detsaw. If we do not give up our plans to move to Neerg, they will attack."

"We cannot give up," said Madra. "Besides, this is a good chance to test our defense systems."

"I really hate tests," I said, but no one paid any attention to me.

Kaylin started counting. "Ten seconds, nine. . . eight. . . seven. . . six. . . five. . . four. . . three. . . two. . . one!"

41

SEVEN

Boom!

These Sloof types didn't waste any time. The ship shook so hard I would have been knocked out of my seat if I hadn't been strapped in.

"The shields are holding," Orlando announced.

"I thought you were going to avoid their weapons," I said when the ship had stopped shaking.

"We are," Orlando told me. "If they had hit us directly we'd be in a million little pieces by now."

"They're closing in," said Kaylin.

"Full right turn," Madra ordered.

I felt the ship lurch sideways. A second later there was another loud boom. This time it seemed farther away and the ship hardly shook at all.

"We're behind them now," said Kaylin. Then, "They're turning around!"

We waited, watching the ship on the screen above Madra.

"It's fast," said Madra, "but big and awkward. We can easily outmaneuver it. Stand by."

It kept coming, like a falcon on a sparrow. I clenched my teeth to keep from yelling, "Do something!"

"Ten seconds," said Kaylin, "nine, eight,"

My heart stopped beating.

"seven, six. . ."

"Full backward somersault," ordered Madra.

My stomach dropped, like it does on a roller coaster. The whole room tipped backward, farther and farther until we were hanging upside down in our chairs. Everyone was deathly quiet. My fingers curled around the arms of the chair. I clenched my teeth to keep from screaming. The ship kept tipping, backward and backward, until it was right side up again.

"We did it!" announced Kaylin. "We're behind them again. They're way too clumsy to catch us and they know it. They're going away!"

"Yahoo!" I shouted, slipping my arms out of the straps and waving them in the air.

Everyone else was very quiet, watching me.

"What is this word, yahoo?" asked Madra. "It is not in our dictionary."

"Well," I said. "It means... it's just something you yell when you're excited and happy."

"Yahoo!" shouted Orlando, waving his arms in the air. He grinned, "That felt good!"

The others all tried it then, waving their arms and shouting. They sounded just like my volleyball team when we win a close game.

The shouting died down and Madra said, "Well done, crew. But now we have got to get ourselves home. Kaylin, watch the Sloof ship in case they circle back. Orlando, keep our defences at ready. Red and Lotus, check the ship for damages."

As Red and Lotus ran out of the room, they seemed to be moving in slow motion. With every step they floated into the air and then landed softly on the floor again.

"I feel funny," I said.

"You are funny," said Kaylin. "That's why we brought you here."

"No, I mean I feel strange. I feel like I could float into the air."

I undid my seatbelts and stood up. But I didn't really stand up–I kind of floated up, right into the air above Kaylin. She looked up at me with her eyes wide. I waved my arms and legs trying to come down but I just floated higher up.

"What are you doing?" Kaylin asked.

"I don't know," I said. "But it's cool. Come on up and try it."

Kaylin bit her lip. She glanced at her computer screen and back up at me. Then she undid her seatbelts and floated out of her chair. She drifted right to me and took my hand. In a minute we were hovering way up at the top of the dome, looking down at the others and grinning.

Zared was still working away at his keyboard. He glanced up at us and then over at Madra. "That first missile destroyed our gravity control," he said. "Our oxygen will not last long either."

"How long have we got?" asked Madra.

"Maybe five minutes."

"See if you can repair it." She looked up at us. "You have got to come down right now," she said. "I need Kaylin to tell me how soon we will hit the atmosphere of Detsaw. Also, you will need oxygen."

She reached over to the speaker beside her and flipped a

switch. "Lotus and Red. Go to the nearest emergency room and strap yourselves to the seats. Be ready to put on your oxygen helmets."

Then she looked back up at us. "Can you get down here?" she asked.

"We're trying," Kaylin told her. "But it feels so weird!"

I was so light that I didn't have any weight at all. My stomach turned upside down. I swallowed. If I threw up, where would it go?

"Try moving like we did outside the ship," said Orlando.

I spread my arms and ducked my head. Nothing happened. I moved my arms and legs but still nothing happened.

"That only worked outside because you were being pulled by the ship," Zared told us. "You will have to push yourself down now. But be careful not to get too far away from the walls of the dome."

With my feet I pushed against the glass and started floating downward. Only it didn't seem like down any more. There was no up or down when there was no gravity. I came to a stop not far above Orlando. He stretched up his arm but couldn't reach me. I had floated away from the walls of the dome. It felt weird to be just hanging there, like one of those big paper cutouts of ourselves we did back in grade two.

"Two minutes of oxygen," said Zared.

I looked for Kaylin and saw her climbing down the side of the dome like a fly on a wall. When she was close to me she reached out and I grabbed her hand. She tried to pull me back, but the glass was smooth and she had nothing to cling to. She floated out toward me. We were hanging above Orlando. He stretched up but couldn't quite reach my hand.

"One minute of oxygen," warned Zared.

"Stay there," said Orlando, "I'll get you down."

He undid his seatbelts and wrapped the end of one around his wrist. Then he floated up until his feet were above his head. With my free hand I managed to grab one of Orlando's ankles as it floated by. Using his seatbelt as an anchor, Orlando pulled all of us down to the floor.

Kaylin let go of my hand and threw her arms around Orlando's neck. "Thank you," she said, "you saved our lives!"

I pulled at her arm. "Let's go." My voice sounded angry and I didn't know why.

Orlando raised his eyebrows and grinned. But when he spoke he was serious enough. "Mark's right," he said. "You've got to put on your helmets, there isn't much time left. Don't let go of the console."

I walked behind Kaylin, hanging onto the edge of the console and trying to keep my feet on the floor. I almost laughed out loud, it felt so weird, but I knew this was no time for laughing. Already I was having trouble breathing. It was the same feeling as I get near the end of a soccer game when I keep pushing myself to run, no matter how tired I am. I took deeper and deeper breaths but couldn't get enough air.

"Zero oxygen," said Zared putting on his helmet. Orlando put his on too.

My heart started thumping hard against my ribs. I felt like throwing my arms in the air and screaming. Kaylin kept on walking

46

in front of me.

"Stay calm," said Madra, in her smooth, soothing voice. "You have plenty of time if you do not panic. Hold your breath as you would if you were swimming."

Stay calm, I told myself. Stay calm, we're almost there. I couldn't hold my breath much longer, my lungs were collapsing in on themselves like old soccer balls with no air left in them. Kaylin reached her chair. Before she sat down she looked at me and smiled. I smiled back and forgot all about my caved-in lungs. Kaylin sat down and started doing up her seatbelts.

I grabbed the arms of my chair, pulled myself down, and did up my seatbelts too. I reached for my helmet and put it on. I took a breath and then another one. But I wasn't getting any air. I started breathing faster and faster. I felt like I was going to pass out. Kaylin tapped on my helmet. She looked at me, folded her hands beside her cheek and closed her eyes. I knew what she was saying. Relax, take it easy, don't panic.

That wasn't easy to do. I closed my eyes and thought about my breathing. I took one slow, easy breath, let it out and took another one. Before long I realized there was plenty of air. More than enough. I remembered what Kaylin had said about the switch near my chin and flipped it over.

"You okay?" asked Kaylin.

"Sure," I said. "I'm fine. What's happening?"

"We're entering the atmosphere of Detsaw. Zared figures we should have a normal landing."

"Good," I said. "I like normal."

Zared was talking on the radio in a language I didn't understand.

"We're circling Detsaw," Kaylin explained. "We made it through the upper atmosphere without a problem. Everything looks good."

"Tell me about your planet."

She sighed. "It used to be beautiful. I remember my grandmother telling me how birds once filled the air with their songs. When she was young she used to go hiking in forests where the trees were green and healthy. People drank water from mountain streams back then, and swam in the lakes and oceans without getting sick."

"What happened?"

"Lots of things." She bit her lip. "Too many people. Too many chemicals. Global warming. At first plants and animals started dying but no one paid much attention. After a while, humans started dying too. Deserts got bigger and people died of thirst. In other places they drowned in flash floods. And the whole planet kept getting warmer and warmer."

"I can't believe it!" I said. "Why didn't someone do something before it was too late?"

Kaylin shook her head. Behind the face plate her eyes were moist. She blinked and looked away. "No one thought everything would die. The world is so big, we didn't think we could kill it."

She was so upset I tried to change the subject. "Are your parents coming to Neerg with you?" She looked down at her hands and paused a minute before answering. "My parents died a few years ago. See, as the planet got warmer people started dying from strange diseases. The older people, like my grandmother, and the really young children, like my, uh, like my little brother, died first.

Then people my parent's age started getting sick. After a while doctors discovered something weird. Some of us–mostly young people–were getting warmer, just like the planet. And the ones who got warmer didn't get sick."

"So that's why you guys all feel so warm! I thought there was something wrong with me!"

Kaylin smiled, a sad, watery smile. "Yes," she said, "you were kind of funny."

"Approaching spaceport," said Zared.

A few minutes later there was a slight bump. The ship wriggled back and forth and then was still.

"Welcome to Detsaw," said Madra. "You can undo your seatbelts now."

EIGHT

The doors slid open and I gazed out on a forested hillside. Soft mist clung to the treetops. At the foot of the hill was a small lake with water as smooth as glass. Everything glowed in a pink-orange light.

"But," I said, "it's beautiful!"

Kaylin walked down the gangway with me. "Wait," she said, "the sun is just coming up."

As the light grew stronger I saw that most of the trees were like skeletons with naked branches reaching out. Some still had needles but, instead of green, they were an ugly, rusty-brown. On other hillsides were no trees at all, only bare, brown rock and a few short stumps.

"We needed the wood for houses and fuel," Kaylin explained. She nodded toward rows of small houses and, at the edge of the lake, a few huge buildings that looked like airplane hangars.

"As far as we know, this was the very last valley to die," Kaylin told me. "We're high up in the mountains, far away from any cities. Anyway, nearly all of Detsaw's big cities were built near the sea so they're underwater now."

"Detsaw must have a lot more water than Neerg."

Kaylin looked at me for a moment as if she wanted to say something. Then she shrugged and looked away. "I guess so."

As we approached the lake I noticed a strange smell. Getting closer I realized the water was thick and green like a big pot of pea soup. "Yuck!" I said, "what a cesspool!"

"We still drink the water," said Kaylin. "It's all we have. But it needs to be boiled for hours."

As the sun moved higher in the sky it became so bright I couldn't keep my eyes open. I put my hand over them.

"Put these on," said Kaylin, handing me some dark glasses. "The chemicals in the air destroyed our protection from the sun. Millions of people went blind before we realized what was wrong."

By then people were coming out of the houses and hurrying toward one of the big buildings. When they passed close to us I noticed that nearly all of them were teenagers and all had green eyes.

"This is Mark, from Neerg," said Kaylin.

They hurried past. "We have got work to do, we will talk later," they said.

"How come you don't needed sunglasses?" I asked Kaylin.

"Did you notice the colour of our eyes?"

I nodded. "Everyone has green eyes, like you. They're pretty."

"Thank you," she smiled. "But they're also very necessary. Those of us who survived have special protection from the sun. Kind of like built-in sunglasses."

"So, if you don't have green eyes and extra warm blood you don't survive on Detsaw?"

"Right."

"Then what happens to me?"

"Don't worry, you'll only be here a few days. We're going to load up the transport ship and the shuttle and head for Neerg. In the evenings before we leave and while we are on the ship you can teach us how to behave like you and your friends."

Just then Red, Orlando and Lotus caught up to us. "We've got problems," said Red.

"What's wrong?" asked Kaylin.

"Zared says there's no way he can fix the shuttle in less than a month."

"If we're really careful, we will have just enough dried food to last," said Lotus.

"What about Mark?" asked Kaylin. "He can't survive that long on Detsaw."

"I'll just stay indoors all the time," I said.

Orlando shook his head. "The heat would get you. Our houses are like ovens and the water, even boiled, will make you sick. We have a little bottled water left from the old days. We kept it for emergencies."

"Okay then, maybe I'm like you. Maybe I won't get sick."

Lotus put her palms together and pressed her fingers against her chin. She looked up at me sadly. "There is something in our immune system that protects us. Dr. Senob tested you after you fainted, you don't have it."

"Then why the heck did you bring me here?"

"We needed your help. It was only supposed to be for a few days. You wouldn't get sick that quickly and we have enough safe water to last almost a week."

I had never thought too much about dying before. Except, of course, when I thought I had already done it. But I knew now I wanted to live and to see Earth again. If I had to die, I didn't want to do it so far away from home on this ugly, lifeless planet.

"Try not to worry," said Kaylin. "We'll think of something."

***

Orlando and Lotus went to help Zared repair the shuttle. I went with Kaylin and Red to the big building that held the transport ship.

Kaylin took me on a tour. Teenagers were working inside and out. Some were welding, some were testing the computers, others were loading food and fuel. Inside the ship were rows and rows of seats and shelves of books. Down below was a hold for storage and at the very top was a room like the domed control room on the shuttle.

"Why don't we all just go to Neerg on this?" I asked Kaylin.

"We could. But the transport ship can't land on Neerg. Can you imagine landing this big thing without being seen?"

"No. You're right. People on Neerg go crazy if they spot a UFO. There's no telling what they might do."

"Right. So we must leave the transport ship in space. We need the shuttle to carry people to different parts of your country."

"Are you going to live near me?" Then I remembered. I might not be going back. "I mean, are you going to be anywhere near the Okanagan?

"No," she said. "I'm not on the list to go to there."

***

Kaylin had work to do so I walked back to the shuttle. I was hoping that by then Zared had discovered it could be fixed up quickly.

People were all around the shuttle, busy working. I found Zared.

"Well," I said. "Can you fix it?"

"Yes," he told me. "But the Sloof ship did more damage than I thought. It will not be safe to travel for more than a month. And we must improve our defense system. By the way, Dr. Senob is looking for you."

Dr. Senob was in his lab. He gave me a checkup and took the bandage off my forehead.

"Well, doc, how long have I got?"

He was looking at a drop of my blood under a microscope. "We can not risk keeping you here more than three days," he said. "But I have an idea." He stood up. "Let us go and find Madra."

We found her working in the command dome.

"What about sending Mark home on the explorer?" Dr. Senob asked.

"Do you think he could handle it?"

54

"It is his only chance," Dr. Senob told her.

"I will talk to Kaylin and the others. They will know if he is capable."

My friends must have thought I could do it, because an hour later I was sitting behind the wheel.

The small, ball shaped craft was hardly big enough for one person. A panel in front of me was filled with dials.

"Do not worry," said Zared. "You do not have to learn what all of them are. I will program the computer to take you right to the swamp across from your home. But you must learn how to land so the explorer will not break up before you get out."

"Okay," I said, fighting down a wave of panic, "teach me."

"When this craft hits your atmosphere it will look like a ball of lightning. It is very fast but it was never made for a long trip and it will burn up quickly. You have time to land and get out if you keep calm and do everything right."

"Just call me Mr. Calm."

Zared sighed and scratched his head. "All right," he said. "Here is what you have to do."

Zared went over and over the landing instructions. Then he left me alone to get the feel of the explorer. "Practice on your own for a while," he said. "You can move the stick and the steering wheel around. You cannot hurt anything."

I stayed there all afternoon.

***

That night I went with Kaylin and the others to an empty building where an earlier transport ship had been built. All the kids on Detsaw came in. They had hundreds of questions.

I tried to tell them about our music and dancing, but I never was much of a dancer. Most of them wanted to know about sports so I told them about volleyball. I figured it was the easiest to start with. We found some string to use for a net and a child's lightweight helmet for a ball. We ripped the foam rubber out of the inside and glued it to the outside.

"There are no more children," said Kaylin, sadly. "So no one will miss it."

They kept getting hit on the head. "Keep your eyes on the ball," I told them over and over.

We set up several more nets. While they practiced I got another group together. "You have to know about hockey," I told them. I explained what a hockey stick looked like.

"I have an idea," said one of the girls.

She ran off and came back with some sticks that looked like canes. "People used these before they died," she told me. "They couldn't walk very well."

We found a roll of black electrician's tape to use for a puck and set up nets using some metal pipes left over from building the transport ship.

We had a great time running up and down and hitting the tape with the canes. Soon we were all laughing. But before long I got so hot I had to take a break. I drank a liter of water.

"Hockey is really played on ice," I explained, wiping my forehead. "And you wear ice skates on your feet."

"We've never seen ice," said Orlando.

"Don't worry," I told him, "you will."

NINE

The next day, for the first time in their lives, all the young people took the day off. I showed them how to play soccer, basketball and baseball. We used all kinds of crazy equipment. They laughed and fooled around just like kids at home. But they had never played any sports before and they were really clumsy. They kept getting hit by the ball.

"Keep your eyes on the ball!" I reminded them, as I watched from the sidelines. The heat was too much for me, there was no way I could run. I sat and gave pointers and drank gallons of water.

In the late afternoon Madra sat down beside me. "This is wonderful," she said. "This is what we brought you here to do. Our young people have never had time to enjoy themselves and you have been good for them. You even showed me how to talk properly. We'll always be grateful.

But I'm afraid you have to leave now, Zared says this is the only safe time to go."

"Now? But I'm having fun! I thought I had another day."

"We cannot control the movements of planets. If you do not go now, you could land in Siberia."

"Okay, I'm ready. Can I just find Kaylin and say good-bye?"

"I'm sorry, she's busy on an errand and there is not enough time."

57

Madra walked with me to the explorer. "There is something you should know. Because our ship travels much faster
than the speed of light, it creates a time warp. When you get
home, it will still be the same night, not much later than when
you left."

"Cool," I said.

'Will you miss your new friends?"

"Yes," I stared at the toes of my running shoes.

"Especially Kaylin?"

"I guess."

"She'll miss you too."

I felt a sudden surge of happiness. Madra was watching
me closely.

"That's okay," I said. "Maybe I'll see her around."

Madra shook her head. "Kaylin will be living in Nova
Scotia with Dr. Senob and a group of young people."

Nova Scotia! I thought. She couldn't get much farther
away.

"Remember, if you meet any of our people on Neerg they
must act as if they never saw you before. No one must know we
are aliens, that would be very dangerous for us."

"I understand," I told her.

***

A few minutes later I was squeezed into the little craft. Zared
looked down at me through the hatch.

"Remember to pull back hard on the stick when you are
exactly 3500 metres from the ground," he said.

58

"I know."

"Keep watching the dial so you'll know when to ease it forward again. Any questions?"

"No."

"OK. Then I want you to tell me everything you are going to do."

I went over every detail for the hundredth time.

"Good. Keep going over it in your head on the way home. Remember, you will forget everything if you panic."

"Who, me? Panic?" I grinned.

Zared sighed and scratched his head.

"Don't worry," I said. "I'll be practicing all the way there."

"Good luck," he reached in and shook my hand. Then I closed the hatch.

A deafening roar surrounded me. The entire craft shuddered with the sound. I gripped the steering wheel and squeezed my eyes shut. The roar got louder and louder until I thought my eardrums would burst. Then, suddenly, it disappeared behind me. An invisible force, like a giant hand, pushed me back against the seat. I couldn't open my eyes. The skin of my face felt as if it were being pushed back around my ears.

Slowly the pressure got less and went away. My arms floated into the air. In the mirror beside me, I watched my hair drifting around my head like it does underwater. I had left Detsaw behind. Next stop, Earth. I pushed a button to open the heat shield in front of me and settled back to watch the stars. I must have fallen asleep because when I looked again there was a beautiful, big planet in front of me. It looked like a half moon.

As the explorer got closer to the planet, it traveled around to the lighted side. The planet began to look like a huge round ball of blue and gray. Closer still, the gray parts became green and brown. I closed the heat shields.

The explorer slowed down as it entered Earth's atmosphere. And then I heard a sizzling sound, like bacon in a hot frying pan. The temperature inside shot up so fast, I started to feel like a piece of bacon in that pan. Sweat spurted out of me. I looked in the mirror to see if I was shriveling up. My face was bright pink and my hair was soaking wet.

The walls around me crackled.

"Fire! I'm on fire! " I screamed.

My heart was pounding so hard against my ribs that I could hardly stand the pain. In a few minutes I would be a little black strip of burnt bacon. Sweat poured into my eyes. I wiped it away with the back of my hand. And then I saw the dial: 7000 meters. The numbers were going down so fast they blurred together. My heart gave an extra beat as it pounded inside my chest and then it seemed to stop for a minute. There was something I was supposed to do.

What?

My hands were slippery with sweat. I rubbed one across my forehead. My brain felt like a block of metal: melting down.

"Who, me? Panic?" Was it really me who said that? And Zared had just sighed and scratched his head. He had reminded me to keep going over his landing instructions on the way home.

There are times in my life when I have wished I was good at following advice. This was one of those times.

Okay. I had to pull myself together. I took one slow, deep breath and looked at the dial.

Five thousand meters. I was supposed to do something at 3500 meters.

I forced myself to breathe slowly, in spite of the crackling in my ears and the deathly heat all around me. "Remember to pull back hard on the stick when you are exactly 3500 meters from the ground."

Zared's words came back into my mind. I grabbed the stick and watched the numbers race by on the dial. Zared had showed me how to pick up on the rhythm so that I would know exactly when to pull back. He had made me practice over and over until I was bored out of my mind. But now I knew what to do.

I watched the numbers until I could count down with them. I couldn't count every number, they were going down too fast. But I could get every tenth one. And so, as it neared 3500 meters I was ready. I counted down, pulled back on the stick and felt a sudden change in the explorer. It was like hitting the brakes on my trail bike.

The numbers on the dial slowed down but the heat kept going up. The metal stick was getting too hot to touch. Then I remembered my gloves and helmet. I reached under the seat for them. With these on and the silver space suit and boots I was wearing, I was fireproof. I would not catch on fire, and I no longer felt like a strip of bacon. No. I felt more like a live crab in a pot of boiling water.

Fear kept grabbing at my stomach and trying to take over my thoughts. But I pushed it away. I wouldn't let it get a hold on me. I knew what I had to do and I was determined to do it.

The numbers on the dial went down to 150 meters. I eased forward on the stick. At 50 meters I started pulling back slowly. The numbers dropped steadily. When the stick was fully back, the dial read one meter. A few seconds later I heard a sound like water being poured onto a burning hot pan. There was a soft bump, the explorer shook, and I had landed.

I had only seconds to get out. But I was ready. The hatch opened easily. I climbed out and threw myself over a ball of flames.

TEN

I landed in slippery, soft muck and sank past my knees in cold water. Flames reached toward me from the burning craft. I tried to run but my boots were buried; stuck deep in the mucky bottom of the swamp. I pulled but they wouldn't come loose. Hot flames licked at my suit. Bending down, I undid the clasps at the top of the boots, yanked my feet out and ran, slipping and sliding in the mud.

My foot sank in a hole and I fell forward. The cool water felt so good on my burning skin that I didn't want to get up. But suddenly I couldn't breathe. I sat up, tore off my gloves, flipped the switches on my helmet, and tossed it into the swamp.

Heat singed the unprotected skin of my hands and neck. Sure that the explorer was about to blow up, I ran as fast as I could, splashing through shallow water to the edge of the swamp. When I looked back, an orange ball of flame was sinking quietly into the dark water.

Water poured off me as I walked across the field toward the lights of my house. I had never been so happy to be home. I raced up the front stairs. The door was locked. I knocked but no one answered, not even Wimp. He must have been hiding. I went around to try the carport door. It was locked too. I was wondering what to do when I heard a car coming. It slowed down and turned into our driveway.

"Mom! Dad!" I shouted as they pulled into the carport. "Am I glad to see you!"

"What on earth have you been doing?" Mom asked, stepping out of the car.

"That's just it, Mom, I wasn't on Earth! I thought I'd never see you again." I ran to hug her.

She stepped back. "You're covered in muck!"

"You can't go into the house like that!" said my father. "What were you doing – crawling around in the swamp?"

"No, Dad, listen . . ."

"It's cold out here," said Mom. "Take off those disgusting coveralls and come inside."

"Don't you see, Mom? It's not coveralls, it's a spacesuit."

Mom and Dad looked at each other. "All right, dear," said Mom as if she were talking to a four year old. "Take off your spacesuit and come inside where it's warm." She turned away and put her hand to her forehead, "I need a cup of tea."

They went inside. I took off my wet, brown spacesuit and wet, brown socks. In the house, I put on some dry clothes and threw the spacesuit into the bathtub to rinse. They would believe me when they saw the shiny silver suit. There was nothing like it on Earth.

Someone pounded on the door.

"Mark!" my mother yelled. "What's this mess in the kitchen?"

Oh-oh. "Sorry, Mom. The lid blew off the popcorn popper. I'll clean it up."

When every piece of popcorn was picked up I sat at the kitchen table with my parents. Mom handed me a mug of hot tea and pushed a plate of chocolate chip cookies at me.

"So," she said, "are you going to tell us what happened?"

"What do you mean?" I asked.

She looked at Dad. He looked at me. "Why did you go out and leave both TVs on? Why was there popcorn all over the floor? What were you doing in the swamp in the middle of the night? And why is Wimp cowering behind my chair in the living room?"

"It's a long story," I said, sipping my tea. "And you might think it's a little hard to believe, but I can prove it."

I leaned back in my chair. "You see, it all started with a big ball of light."

I told them the whole story. When I had finished they just sat there, staring at me.

"Is that the best you can do?" Mom finally asked.

"If you ask me," said Dad. "I think it's a pretty good story. It's better than I could do."

"But it's true," I insisted. "And I can prove it!"

I ran into the bathroom where the spacesuit was soaking and rubbed some of the mud off of it. The silver must have come off with the mud. Underneath it was a plain, dirty white, like the coveralls I wear when I work on my trail bike.

"That's your proof?" my mother stood behind me, looking down. She touched my forehead.

"What happened to your head?"

"Nothing," I said. "It's just a bump."

My father came into the bathroom, he put his arm around my mom's shoulders. They turned and walked out.

"What about the school psychologist?" I heard my dad whisper.

"Maybe he's just overtired. You know with school and the volleyball tournament and playing soccer?" She sighed.

***

I didn't say any more about my trip to Detsaw. When my parents took Wimp for a walk the next day I headed over to the swamp to see if I could find anything. I waded into the cold, dirty water trying to figure out where the explorer had come down. But there was no sign of it, I guess it burned right down to nothing.

I sloshed up and down in the water looking for my helmet, gloves and boots. My foot hit against something, I bent down to feel with my hands. It was rounded, like a helmet, and it felt like metal. I pulled it out of the muck.

"Hey, Mark!"

I forgot Richard was coming over today. "Hi, Richard!" I called and waved to him.

"What are you doing in there?"

I looked down at my hands. I was holding a rusty old tin bucket. I looked back at Richard. We had been friends since we were little kids, but for some reason he didn't always believe everything I said. I threw the bucket away and started wading out of the swamp.

"Nothing," I said.

Richard and I set to work on my trail bike. "Do you believe in UFOs?" I asked him after a while.

"Sure," he said, "doesn't everyone?"

"I mean real spaceships that come and land here on Neerg."

"Neerg?"

"Earth, I meant Earth. So, do you?"

"What?"

"Believe in spaceships."

"I guess so."

"What about Aliens?"

"You mean like little green men?"

"No, not exactly. Not just men and not green–except their eyes. I'm talking about people who look just like us only they come from another planet."

Richard put down the wrench. He stood up and punched me on the arm, grinning. "I'm not stupid, you know."

"What?"

"I know this is one of your dumb jokes."

"Forget it," I said. "Let's get this bike back together."

***

I was beginning to wonder if my parents were right. Maybe I had dreamed the whole thing. Or, maybe there was something wrong with my mind. Either way it would mean that Detsaw did not exist. And if Detsaw didn't exist then Kaylin didn't exist either. I refused to believe that. Kaylin, Madra, the other kids, all of them were very real. Maybe I would never see any of them again, but for sure I would never forget them.

ELEVEN

"Mark Jensen, please come to the office," a voice crackled through the speaker above the chalkboard. Only Monday morning and already I was in trouble.

When I walked into the office, Dr. Jones, the school shrink, was waiting for me. He peered at me under his long, bushy eyebrows. "I'd like to have a talk if that's, ah, all right with you."

"Sure," I said. I wondered what would happen if I said no.

I followed him to his office. He lowered himself onto a comfortable armchair behind his desk and I sat across from him, perched on a straight-backed wooden chair.

"Your parents seem rather, ah, concerned about, ah, you."

I waited to be sure he was finished. He always talked so slowly that it made me want to finish his sentences for him, just to get it over with.

He was watching me, under his eyebrows, so I assumed he was done. I shrugged. "Why?"

"Suppose you, ah, tell me."

"How would I know?"

"I think it has something to do with, ah, Saturday night."

"Saturday?" I tried to look surprised. "Don't tell me they believed that story I told them?"

"I don't know. Suppose you, ah, tell it to me."

I shook my head. "I don't remember. It was just a dream."

Dr. Jones called me in again the next day, but I refused to tell him a thing.

"I can't believe everyone is making such a big deal over a stupid dream," I told my parents that night.

"You haven't gone sleepwalking like that since you were four," said my mother. "And you were wandering around in the swamp, alone, with no shoes on. Don't you think that's scary?"

"Yeah," I said. "I guess."

If I really had been wandering around in the swamp without knowing it, then yes, it would be really scary. But I couldn't be sure. My mind kept going one way and then the other. Sometimes I was convinced the whole thing had happened, just as I remembered it. Other times I was equally certain I had dreamed the whole thing. The only part I couldn't figure out was when I had fallen asleep. It had to be after I went downstairs because both TVs were on when I got home. It also had to be after I made the popcorn. The thing is, if I walked out the door in my sleep, how come both doors were locked when I got back?

***

My mother insisted on sending me to the family doctor.

"But why?" I asked her. "Can't you just forget about that dream? I'm sure it won't happen again."

"It was more than just a dream," she said. "You were sleepwalking. And you've got that funny lump on your forehead."

The doctor touched my forehead. "How did you get that bump?" he asked.

"I hit it when I fell."

"And how did you fall?"

"It was just after I got," ... *transported*. I wiped my forehead

69

with the back of my hand and started again. "It was just after I made some popcorn and it shot all over the room. I slipped on it and hit my head on the kitchen floor."

"Well, there's your answer."

He told me a whole bunch of junk about head injuries. "I once had a patient who wandered around town for days after a head injury. The police finally found him singing in the bandshell at the park. He thought he was an opera star."

The doctor chuckled. I grinned, but I felt like crying. If he was right then none of it was real–not even Kaylin.

***

I had almost forgotten about my crazy dream by the time basketball season started in January. One morning I went to school early to practice. Richard was already there. He walked into the change room.

"Wait till you see these two new guys," he said. "I don't know where they come from but they want to try out for the team. They're pretty good."

We went into the gym and ran over to practice some shots with them. The first guy turned around. He was tall with black curly hair, dark skin and deep, green eyes. I couldn't help it, I reached out and touched him on the shoulder. "You're warm!"

He looked at me strangely. "Been workin' out," he said.

I turned to look at the other guy. He was short and stocky with blond hair and–green eyes!

"Look out!" yelled Richard.

The ball bounced off my head.

"You've got to keep your eyes on the ball," said the shorter player, smiling slightly.

I stared at him. And then I rubbed my head where the ball had hit me. "I don't feel so good," I said. "I think I'll quit for today."

I got changed and walked outside to sit on the cold, stone steps. The sun was low in the sky and a thin layer of snow covered the ground.

"Brrr," said a girl coming up the steps. "It's going to be hard to get used to this cold weather."

I looked down and my heart gave an extra beat. "I thought you were going to Nova Scotia."

The girl glanced around to see if I was talking to someone else, but no one else was there. As she turned back to me, I studied her face.

She looked a lot like Kaylin but her hair was longer and she was much thinner. Too thin, I thought. Her face looked different too. Her cheeks were pink and she seemed happier than Kaylin had ever been. She didn't have the worried look that lurked behind Kaylin's eyes and made her seem older than she really was. This girl was wearing jeans and a warm jacket.

"Hi," she said. "I'm Kelly. And my uncle did want me to move to Nova Scotia with him. But I decided to come here with my Aunt Maggie instead. How did you know about that?"

She had reached the top of the stairs by then. I stood up beside her, she was just a little shorter than me.

"Just a guess," I told her, "you remind me of someone I used to know. Anyway, I sure hope you'll like it here."

She smiled at me and her green eyes sparkled. "I'm pretty sure I will," she said.